GOOD SPORTS, WIN OR LOSE

By BREANN RUMSCH
Illustrated by MIKE PETRIK
Music by MARK MALLMAN

CANTATA
LEARNING

WWW.CANTATALEARNING.COM

CANTATA LEARNING

Published by Cantata Learning
1710 Roe Crest Drive
North Mankato, MN 56003
www.cantatalearning.com

Library of Congress Cataloging-in-Publication Data
Names: Rumsch, BreAnn, 1981– author. | Petrik, Mike, illustrator. | Mallman,
   Mark, musician.
Title: Good sports, win or lose / by BreAnn Rumsch ; illustrated by Mike
   Petrik ; music by Mark Mallman.
Description: North Mankato, Minnesota : Cantata Learning, [2019] | Series:
   Good Sports | Audience: Ages: 5–7. | Audience: Grades: K to Grade 3. |
   "This text is set to the tune of "Here We Go Looby Loo""--T.p. verso. |
   Includes bibliographical references.
Identifiers: LCCN 2018053373 (print) | LCCN 2018056790 (ebook) | ISBN
   9781684104185 (eBook) | | ISBN 9781684104031 (hardcover) | ISBN
   9781684104307 (paperback)
Subjects: LCSH: Sportsmanship--Juvenile literature. | Winning and losing.
Classification: LCC GV706.3 (ebook) | LCC GV706.3 .R864 2019 (print) | DDC
   175--dc23
LC record available at https://lccn.loc.gov/2018053373

Book design and art direction: Tim Palin Creative
Editorial direction: Kellie M. Hultgren
Music direction: Elizabeth Draper
Music arranged and produced by Mark Mallman

Printed in the United States of America.
0406

This text is set to the tune of "Here We Go Looby Loo."

ACCESS THE MUSIC!

SCAN CODE WITH MOBILE APP

CANTATALEARNING.COM

TIPS TO SUPPORT LITERACY AT HOME

WHY READING AND SINGING WITH YOUR CHILD IS SO IMPORTANT

Daily reading with your child leads to increased academic achievement. Music and songs, specifically rhyming songs, are a fun and easy way to build early literacy and language development. Music skills correlate significantly with both phonological awareness and reading development. Singing helps build vocabulary and speech development. And reading and appreciating music together is a wonderful way to strengthen your relationship.

READ AND SING EVERY DAY!

TIPS FOR USING CANTATA LEARNING BOOKS AND SONGS DURING YOUR DAILY STORY TIME

1. As you sing and read, point out the different words on the page that rhyme. Suggest other words that rhyme.

2. Memorize simple rhymes such as Itsy Bitsy Spider and sing them together. This encourages comprehension skills and early literacy skills.

3. Use the questions in the back of each book to guide your singing and storytelling.

4. Read the included sheet music with your child while you listen to the song. How do the music notes correlate to the words of the song?

5. Sing along on the go and at home. Access music by scanning the QR code on each Cantata book. You can also stream or download the music for free to your computer, smartphone, or mobile device.

Devoting time to daily reading shows that you are available for your child. Together, you are building language, literacy, and listening skills.

Have fun reading and singing!

Everybody likes to win! Nobody likes to lose. But we all do a little of both. When we win, we might want to **brag** about it so others are happy for us. When we lose, we might want to be mean to the winners to make ourselves feel better. But both of these things can make the game less fun for everyone.

Win or lose, good sports show **respect** to all players. That means helping everyone feel good about playing. To find out what happens when some basketball players have big feelings about winning and losing, turn the page and sing along!

5

Sometimes our team will win.
Sometimes our team will lose.

We're kind, and we play our best.
Respect is what we choose!

A win feels really great,
unless someone gets mad.

When some players frown and **boo**,
it makes our whole team sad.

9

Sometimes our team will win.
Sometimes our team will lose.

We're kind, and we play our best.
Respect is what we choose!

11

Nobody likes to lose.

The other team has won.

It hurts when the winners brag.

It takes out all the fun.

Sometimes our team will win.
Sometimes our team will lose.

We're kind, and we play our best.
Respect is what we choose!

We feel sad that we lost,
but it was fun to play.

We know that we did our best.
We'll win another day!

Sometimes our team will win.
Sometimes our team will lose.

We're kind, and we play our best.
Respect is what we choose!

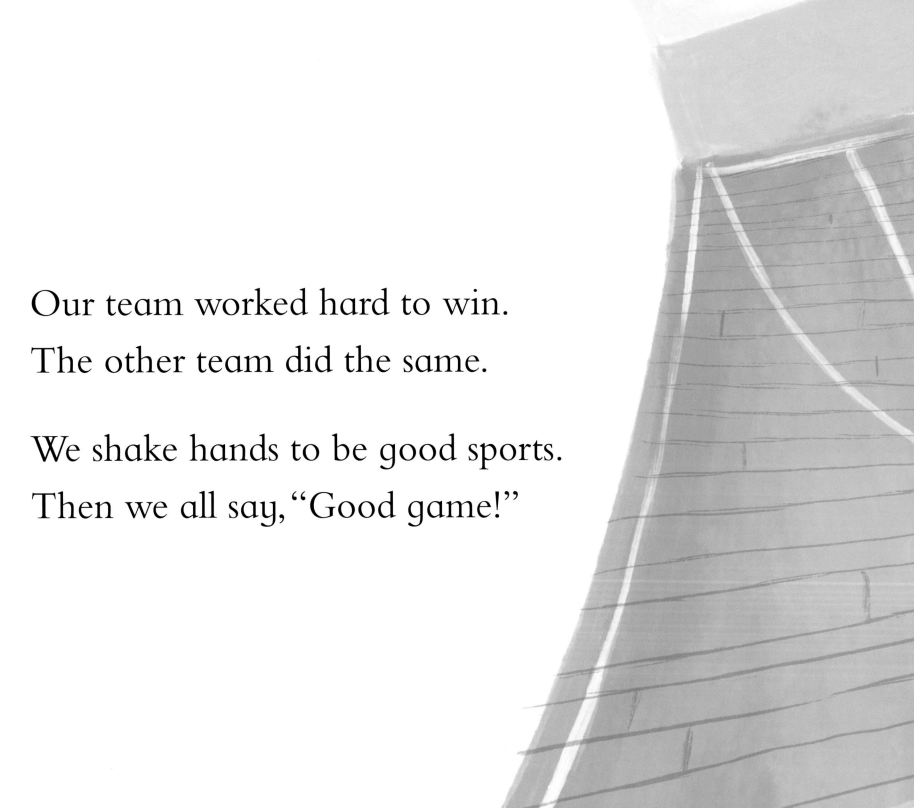

Our team worked hard to win.
The other team did the same.

We shake hands to be good sports.
Then we all say, "Good game!"

21

SONG LYRICS
Good Sports, Win or Lose

Sometimes our team will win.
Sometimes our team will lose.
We're kind, and we play our best.
Respect is what we choose!

A win feels really great,
unless someone gets mad.
When some players frown and boo,
it makes our whole team sad.

Sometimes our team will win.
Sometimes our team will lose.
We're kind, and we play our best.
Respect is what we choose!

Nobody likes to lose.
The other team has won.
It hurts when the winners brag.
It takes out all the fun.

Sometimes our team will win.
Sometimes our team will lose.
We're kind, and we play our best.
Respect is what we choose!

We feel sad that we lost,
but it was fun to play.
We know that we did our best.
We'll win another day!

Sometimes our team will win.
Sometimes our team will lose.
We're kind, and we play our best.
Respect is what we choose!

Our team worked hard to win.
The other team did the same.
We shake hands to be good sports.
Then we all say, "Good game!"

Good Sports, Win or Lose

Hip Hop
Mark Mallman

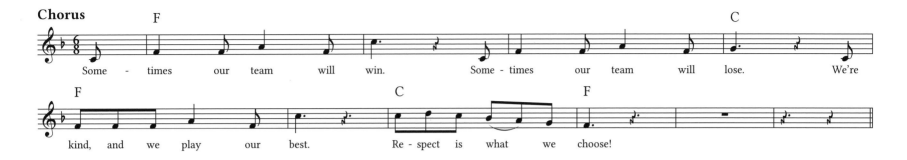

Chorus

Some - times our team will win. Some - times our team will lose. We're
kind, and we play our best. Re - spect is what we choose!

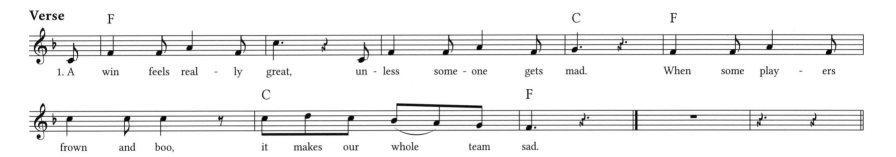

Verse

1. A win feels real - ly great, un - less some - one gets mad. When some play - ers
frown and boo, it makes our whole team sad.

Chorus

Verse 2
Nobody likes to lose.
The other team has won.
It hurts when the winners brag.
It takes out all the fun.

Chorus

Verse 3
We feel sad that we lost,
but it was fun to play.
We know that we did our best.
We'll win another day!

Chorus

Verse 4
Our team worked hard to win.
The other team did the same.
We shake hands to be good sports.
Then we all say, "Good game!"

GLOSSARY

boo—to yell "boo" when unhappy about something in a game

brag—to talk about doing something well, especially in a way that makes others feel bad

respect—a feeling that someone or something is important and should be valued

CRITICAL THINKING QUESTIONS

1. Do you think there is a difference between wanting to play well and wanting to win? What is the difference?

2. It's okay to feel bad about losing. And it's okay to feel happy about winning. But it's not okay to hurt others when those feelings get strong. Draw a picture of of a time when you won or lost. What did it feel like? Draw another picture of what you think someone on the other side felt like.

3. We all win and lose sometimes. Split a piece of paper into two columns and write "Win" and "Lose" at the top. Make a list of the ways a good sport can handle winning. Now make a list of the ways a good sport can handle losing.

TO LEARN MORE

Arrow, Emily. *Making It Happen*. North Mankato, MN: Cantata Learning, 2020.

Doeden, Matt. *All About Basketball*. North Mankato, MN: Capstone, 2015.

Fergus, Maureen. *The Day Dad Joined My Soccer Team*. Toronto, ON: Kids Can, 2018.

Omoth, Tyler. *First Source to Basketball: Rules, Equipment, and Key Playing Tips*. North Mankato, MN: Capstone, 2016.

Pfister, Marcus. *You Can't Win Them All, Rainbow Fish*. New York: North-South, 2017.